D1356146

The Silly Willy Billy Goats

For Lowell Fachau,
With Seriously Silly wishes,
L.S. & A.R.

Visit Laurence Anholt's website at
www.anholt.co.uk

ORCHARD BOOKS
338 Euston Road
London NW3 3BH
Orchard Books Australia
Level 17-207 Kent Street, Sydney, NSW 2000, Australia

First published by Orchard Books in 2008
First paperback publication in 2009

A CIP catalogue record for this book is available from the British Library.

ISBN 978 1 84616 075 2 (hardback)
ISBN 978 1 84616 313 5 (paperback)

1 2 3 4 5 6 7 8 9 10 (hardback)
1 2 3 4 5 6 7 8 9 10 (paperback)

Printed in China

Orchard Books is a division of Hachette Children's Books,
an Hachette Livre UK company.
www.hachettelivre.co.uk

Laurence Anholt   Arthur Robins

seriously SILLY colour

The Silly Willy Billy Goats

ORCHARD BOOKS

Once upon a toilet
in a stinky dump under a bridge,
lived a grumpy old Troll.

He was the grumpiest, dumpiest, lumpiest Troll you could ever hope NOT to meet.

When somebody crossed his bridge,
the Troll would swear like this:

. . . trolley!!

Then he would eat them,
wheels and all. Like this:

Crunch, nice lunch!!

Of course, the Troll
had no friends at all.

Now, on the other side of the bridge, in a green valley sprinkled with daisies, lived three silly goats.

Their names were

Big Tough
Billy Goat Gruff,

tinkley!

Nanny the
Granny

clonky!!

and
Sid the Kid,

CLANK!!!

but everybody called
them the Silly Willy Billy Goats.

The Silly Willy Billy Goats
loved to kid around.

The Silly Willy Billy Goats
loved to play the goat.

One day the Silly Willy Billy Goats were having a big daisy breakfast, when Sid the Kid had an idea.

From under the bridge, the horrible Troll could hear the goats giggling and gaggling and planning Sid's party.

It made him MORE GRUMPY THAN EVER.

Sid the Kid made some party invitations. It took a long time because the goats had LOTS of friends.

Then he set off to deliver the invitations.

Sid the Kid went across the bridge: *Trippety, trap!*
Out came the Troll.

But Sid the Kid was very clever.
He reached in his sack and
pulled out an invitation.
He gave it to the Troll. It said:

Sorry to butt in!
The Silly Willy Billy Goats
are having a PARTY
and YOU are invited

WHERE: Daisy field
near the Trolls place.
WHEN: Teatime until
half past breakfast.
Dress:
Something silly.

The Troll looked at the invitation.

I will come to the party and **I will eat the party boy!**

he roared.

Sid the Kid went quickly on his way and gave invitations to all his friends.

21

All day long the goats got ready
for Sid the Kid's party.
But Sid the Kid was worried.

I am the party boy
and the Troll
will eat me
for his tea.

he bleated.

But Big Tough Billy Goat
Gruff had a plan.

Don't worry, Sid,
I have a
TROLL TRICK!

he giggled.

Soon the guests began to arrive.
Everybody had a silly time.

The last person to arrive was the Troll. He heard music. He saw a lot of people. He was looking forward to eating the party boy.

Then the Troll saw a great big sign. It said:

Happy Birthday, dear Troll.
Welcome to YOUR party!
Ha ha ha! YOU are the party boy! Now you will have to eat yourself.

Then the Troll began to cry.

Don't cry, Troll. You don't **really** have to eat yourself. We were only **kidding.**

I am only crying because I am so happy. No one has ever given me a party.

Then the Troll began to dance.
He danced the Lumpy Dumpy
Belly Dance.

Everybody had a silly time.
The Troll was silliest of all.

He met a beautiful girl Troll.
They danced till dawn . . .

And he
hardly ate
anyone at all.

Laurence Anholt   Arthur Robins
seriously SILLY colour

ENJOY ALL THESE
SERIOUSLY SILLY STORIES!

Bleeping Beauty	ISBN 978 1 84616 073 8
The Elves and the Storymaker	ISBN 978 1 84616 074 5
The Silly Willy Billy Goats	ISBN 978 1 84616 075 2
The Ugly Duck Thing	ISBN 978 1 84616 076 9
Freddy Frog Face	ISBN 978 1 84616 077 6
Handsome and Gruesome	ISBN 978 1 84616 078 3
The Little Marzipan Man	ISBN 978 1 84616 079 0
The Princess and the Tree	ISBN 978 1 84616 080 6

All priced at £8.99

Orchard books are available from all good bookshops, or can be ordered direct from the publisher:
Orchard Books, PO BOX 29, Douglas IM99 1BQ
Credit card orders please telephone: 01624 836000 or fax: 01624 837033
or visit our website: www.orchardbooks.co.uk or e-mail: bookshop@enterprise.net for details.

To order please quote title, author and ISBN and your full name and address.
Cheques and postal orders should be made payable to 'Bookpost plc.'
Postage and packing is FREE within the UK (overseas customers should add £1.00 per book).

Prices and availability are subject to change.